Sisi Elani

Pippa Goodhart

Illustrated by Jane Bottomley

OXFORD

UNIVERSITY PRESS

OXFORD
UNIVERSITY PRESS

Great Clarendon Street, Oxford OX2 6DP

Oxford University Press is a department of the University of Oxford.
It furthers the University's objective of excellence in research, scholarship,
and education by publishing worldwide in

Oxford   New York

*Athens Auckland Bangkok Bogotá Buenos Aires Cape Town
Chennai Dar es Salaam Delhi Florence Hong Kong Istanbul Karachi
Kolkata Kuala Lumpur Madrid Melbourne Mexico City Mumbai Nairobi
Paris São Paulo Shanghai Singapore Taipei Tokyo Toronto Warsaw*

with associated companies in *Berlin Ibadan*

Oxford is a registered trade mark of Oxford University Press in the UK and
in certain other countries

ISBN 0 19 919273 1

For my beautiful sister,
Joey

The
True Journal
of
Druscilla
Overton

1st June

It is night time. The street outside is dark and quiet. The house and mill around me are quiet, but my head is noisy with thoughts churning and grinding like the wheels and cogs of the mill, thinking of the past and the future and I cannot settle.

Tansy lies beside me, fast asleep and with her thumb in her mouth even though she is nine years old. Even if she were awake I could not talk to her, or to anybody else, about how I feel.

Tansy is happy and I do not want to disturb that. Mother needs to think that all is well and, at fifteen, I am too old to go crying to her. So I shall write my feelings into this book.

Father always said that he could sort out his problems by shaping them into the furniture he made. He said that working wood was a kind of conversation, him and the wood deciding the shape of things together. I hope that writing in this book will be like a conversation too. I hope that Father's old book and I between us can make sense of my new stepsister, Ella.

This big book was given to Father on the day he completed his apprenticeship as a cabinet maker. It has his name – Master Abel Overton – and his trade – Master Cabinet Maker – written in curly script on the front page. It was his daybook, recording the ordering of wood and wax and varnish, and the selling of finished furniture. It records money spent and money earned, but it also records something of our family life.

There in Father's familiar, ink splattered writing, is the entry for the bridal bed that he made for his marriage to Mother. There is the cradle made for my birth, and the low nursing chair made as a gift for Mother when Tansy was born. Noah's Ark is there, and each of the animals Father carved to be added to the ark every Christmas.

There too, is the tiny coffin Father made for our baby brother who lived only one day. The book records the comings and goings of work and of life. Then Father's writing suddenly stops for his own life had ended.

After that there are a few lines in Mother's less sure hand, noting the sale of some of our family furniture, sold to buy food and coal after Father died. Then white, blank pages, like life, going on and waiting to be filled without Father. Well, I am going to live and fill those pages, and tell more of our family story.

2nd June

After Father died, Mother, Tansy and I lived on in our old home, although it no longer felt like home without Father. Mother took in fine sewing and sold some furniture. Tansy and I worked the garden and cared for the hens. But all of us quietly wondered what would happen when there was no more of Father's fine furniture to sell.

Then one day, as Mother and Tansy queued for bread, Miller Trower happened to be delivering sacks of flour to the bakery. His work had dusted him, head to toe, in flour. Tansy caught sight of him and screamed fit to scare anyone because she thought the miller was a ghost! Miller Trower, being a kindly man, came forward to show Tansy that he was a man and not a ghost.

Tansy clung to Mother's skirts as he spoke to her, and that is how Mother and Miller Trower got to laugh together and become acquainted.

Miller Trower's wife died seventeen years ago,

in the hours after giving birth to his daughter, Ella. Since then, Papa Miller and Ella have lived on at the mill, helped by a housekeeper called Martha.

But now, Papa Miller and Mother have married and Martha has gone to live with her ailing sister.

Mother wore flowers in her brown hair in church – five red roses from the mill garden, one for each of us who will form a new family together. She mixed the roses with bright blue forget-me-nots to show that she has not forgotten Father.

She and Papa Miller looked so happy together, arm in arm. Both of them now has a second parent for their daughters. But we daughters are less sure of the new arrangements.

My new stepsister, Ella, is beautiful. In church yesterday I heard people admiring her and

wondering whether she might be the next bride to walk down that aisle.

She behaved prettily in church, but once we were back at the mill and the door closed on the outside world, Ella took hold of me by my shoulder and pushed me into the grain store. She spat words at me and her arms spun like windmill sails.

'You must understand that you and your ugly little sister are never, never to call my father "Papa"! He is my papa, not yours, and not your coarse, ugly mother's!'

'Mother is not coarse!' I told Ella. 'And she is certainly good enough to marry your father!'

'My real mama was so beautiful she could have married any man she chose,' said Ella. But I have seen the previous Mistress Trower's miniature portrait and she had teeth that stuck out like a rabbit's. 'Before Papa brought you here, we had Martha to cook and clean for us. She treated me properly. She called me Miss Ella and told me that one day I should marry a fine wealthy man and that I would never have to sweep the hearth and blacken my hands as she did. Martha understood me! You common country people never will, never!'

I could see tears welling in Ella's eyes, and she saw me see the tears.

She gave me such a look of hatred, then she turned on her heel and slammed out of the room. I could hear her shoes racing up the stairs to the attic.

I was so angry with Ella for speaking of Mother in that way that I kicked and punched the grain sacks around me, then I wrenched open the door and shouted up the stairs, 'Nobody will ever want to marry you, Ella

Trower. You are too bad tempered and lazy to be loved!' I did not think that Ella would have heard me, but she did. She shouted back, 'Well, if nobody marries me, it will be your fault!'

3rd June

I tried to tell Mother something of Ella's spite, but Mother put a hand on my arm. 'Ella misses her mama . . .'

'How is that? She never knew her mama!'

But Mother shook her head. 'It is quite possible to miss what you have never had. Ella misses the mama she imagines her own to have been. She resents my marrying her father for her dead mama's sake. She is also frightened that she has to share her father with us now. She has only ever had her papa entirely to herself.'

'But we won't . . .'

'To be sure, we won't. In time Ella will learn that she is still loved as she always has been. She is only as you were, Silla, at the age of six when your sister was born. You went back to acting like a baby to try to equal little Tansy's charms for your father and me. You were quite horrid for a time! We must be patient with poor Ella.'

'But . . . !' I began. Mother put a finger to my lips.

'Patience!' she said.

'Patience,' I thought. That is a word sometimes used as a girl's name, and now I have a new thought in my head. Might Mother and Papa Miller have babies of their own? Might there be more sisters, or even a son, to knock Ella further from her place as adored daughter? I feel sure that she has thought of that. She has certainly heard the chatter in town, wondering when she might marry and leave home. It is no surprise that she feels that she is being pushed out. Mother is probably right. I must be patient with Ella and try to make friends with her. Tansy and I might need a friend if a new baby were to come into the house!

9th June

We have lived in the mill for over a week now.
Once more Tansy is softly snoring beside me in
the bed we share. I can hear creaking noises
from the room above that is now Ella's room.
She too must be awake.

Miller Trower had Martha's old room livened
up with a new window and whitewash to make
a new bedroom for Ella. It smells of new wood
up there, the smell of Father's workshop. The
new room is fine, even having wallpaper on one
wall as if it was the drawing room. I would love
such a place to myself, but Ella is in a sulk about
it. She has passed this, her old room, to Tansy
and me – the 'two ugly dumplings from the

country' as she calls us.

I offered to move to the bright new attic room, but instantly Ella changed her mind and decided to take the new room after all. 'Even though I shall be in the attic as if I were a servant,' she said. I never knew of a servant with wallpaper on her wall!

This room still smells of Ella's lavender water. It does not feel as if it belongs to Tansy and me in spite of the little table brought from home along with our dear old Noah's Ark.

Flour dust has settled on the table already. Flour dust is everywhere in this mill house, just as sawdust powdered our old home. Perhaps when flour dust has settled on us all we will feel at home.

Our old home was in the country, and thoroughly dark at this time of night. I don't know whether I shall like living in town. There are shouts and noises from the sea front and I hear running footsteps and feel that I must look from the window and see who is passing by so late. There are sounds too from the bakery next

door where already they are preparing the dough for tomorrow's bread. I like the yeast-scented air and spicy warmth of Baker Reuben's place. He is Miller Trower's great friend and best customer.

Baker Reuben's apprentice, Alfred Hopkiss, is in love with Ella. He looks at her with big eyes and a silly grin on his face. But Ella is scornful of him. 'He is trade!' she says, seeming to forget that her own father is 'trade' too. She thinks she is far too grand for 'trade', although why she objects to those using their skills to make a living I cannot imagine.

Her Ladyship, Miss Eleanor Trower sees herself as gentry, lazily watching as others do the work of the day. She fancies herself dressed in embroidered silk with her waist squashed tight by whalebone corsets. Think of those poor great whales, the last creatures you could ever imagine wearing a corset, being turned into such things!

Worse than that, Ella wants to shave off her hair! Ella's hair is truly beautiful, golden and shiny like new harvested grain. How can she

want to be bald? She says that all the grand folk are bald these days. It is the fashion.

They wear wigs of somebody else's hair, or even horse hair. Wigs are smelly, wobbly, scratchy things that need powdering with flour that must surely turn to paste when it rains. I think they are mad! Ella even wants poor Papa Miller to wear a wig, but he laughs at that!

'And how would I work in the mill in a dratted wig? It would get knocked over my eyes whenever I hefted a sack of grain onto my shoulders!'

Ella told him that he could take the wig off at home or at work and leave it on a wig stand.

'And feel the cold draught over my head?'

'No, Papa!' said Ella as if her father were a little simple. 'Then you wear bed caps and smoking hats and . . .'

'I think I'll keep my head as the good Lord intended,' said Miller. 'I've no time for fussing with wigs, nor money to spare on hats for this, that and t'other. The whole thing is a nonsense. Why, you'll be saying that the cats should shave and wear hats next!' Papa Miller and Mother laughed together.

Ella's eyes turned hard and shiny as rock toffee and she turned and left the room, crashing the door behind her. I know what she is thinking. Ella is thinking that if Mother had not been there, then Miller might well have done as she told him. She has made him do things before. She persuaded him to buy snuff and to try the fashionable bitter taste of coffee.

I notice that Ella does not suggest that Mother should wear a wig. She is of the opinion that Mother is too common to consider fashion. I say that she has too much common sense for it!

23rd September

Ella does care achingly about how she appears to all in society except her own family. She is content to tantrum like a small child at home, with no care at all for what we might think. Yet she worries desperately what every other person in the kingdom might think of her. She passes the day moping around the house. She sighs, then throws herself down on chairs, then flounces off to her room where I suspect she spends a great deal of time gazing into the looking glass that Papa Miller gave her.

Mother tried suggesting that at seventeen Ella is now easily of an age when she might work. She could be apprenticed to the milliner in town and earn a little money that way. Think of the fashionable hats that she could create for herself! Mother thought that style of work would suit Ella very well. But Ella was indignant at the suggestion.

'I am not some lower class girl who must work, Mistress Overton!' She always calls Mother that. She won't try Dorothy, or even Mistress Trower as Mother now is. 'I see no reason why I should slave to support you and your daughters!'

'Nobody is asking you to slave, Ella, but you should do your share,' Mother told her. 'Tansy sweeps the floors and makes beds and helps with the cooking. And Silla does even more, sewing at home and earning treats at the bakery.'

I enjoy my work at the bakery. I help to stone and wash the mountains of currants and raisins. I pound and sieve the great tall loaves of sugar. Today Alfred and I were blanching almonds. They are for Baker Reuben to turn into almond paste.

My fingers are red and tender from fishing the floating nuts from the boiling water and squeezing them out of their skins. Squeezed carefully and fast, the nuts will shoot like a bullet from a pistol and go quite a distance.

Alfred shot one further than mine but I could not try to equal it for Baker Reuben came into the room at that moment. I shall beat him the next time, though! I do enjoy the warmth from the ovens and the chatter at the bakery, particularly when Ella is making things frosty as home. When I pound and knead the thick, yeasty bread dough, I sometimes imagine it is Ella. I thump it with such energy it makes Alfred laugh at me, but I feel better for it. I earn a few pennies and bring home cakes and bread. And sometimes there are pastries which Alfred has spoiled on purpose so that they cannot be sold and he can send them home with me for Ella. Ella eats them, of course, but refuses to like Alfred for his kind presents.

So I earn my way while Ella, who is older, does nothing. I am afraid that I am forever bringing that fact to Mother's notice, and now even Mother's patience with Ella is wearing thin. She is taking my side in things at last. She told Ella, 'It is time that you made some contribution to the upkeep of this family.'

Ella huffed and puffed and waved her arms in the air and said, 'I suppose you want me to . . . to clean the fire grates and ruin my few poor gowns with cinders. As if I were a common maid!'

'No,' said Mother in her quiet voice. Ella does not yet understand that Mother's quiet voice is the one to beware of. 'You shall cover your clothes with a smock and clean the grates carefully so as not to spill the cinders.'

'Father would not hear of me doing such a task!' declared Ella, stamping her foot. 'Father?' Miller Trower shuffled and his face went pink, but he told Ella that she must do as her stepmother ordered.

So Ella went into the drawing room and cleared the grate there for the first time in her life.

Tansy came and told me, big-eyed, that she'd peeped around the door and seen Ella spotting a dot of soot onto her face with one finger.

'Is Ella going to pretend to be ill?' asked

Tansy. But my guess is that Ella was giving herself a black dot on her upper lip or her cheek to be a beauty spot. That is another fashion she is anxious to follow. Where is the beauty in a black spot? Will I understand these things and do them myself when I get to be seventeen and old enough to go courting? I hope not.

Tansy is snuggled close to me as I write. She clings a little at the moment. She is made unhappy as we all are by the shouting with Ella. It is hard enough to lose a father and move to a new home and a new dame school without all this upset as well.

Mother tries to pretend that we are all happy, but we are not.

Will we ever be? Why does Ella have to hate us so? We are all jumpy as fleas in case she starts shouting again. She is not a lady, whatever she thinks. And neither is she pretty when she is frowning and sulky. Her unhappiness drags us all down.

I pray she shall cheer up soon.

1st April

My prayer has been answered in the most surprising way! A grand footman in a powdered wig came to the door. Mother wiped her floury hands on her apron and took a folded and sealed paper from him. It is an invitation from the King! Fancy such a thing!

The King is holding a grand ball in celebration of the coming of age of Prince Gabriel. He has the curious notion that he will invite all manner of people to the ball.

The talk in the baker's shop is that the King worries about his son. The Prince has only ever met grand leisured people from the life at court. The King thinks that a future monarch should

know more about his
people if he is to rule
them wisely and
well. So the King
has invited gentlemen
from every corner
of his kingdom.
He has asked
people from
every trade and
profession – farmers, doctors,
merchants, sea captains . . .
everyone. And Baker Reuben and Miller Trower
have been invited to attend, together with their
families.

'So I am to go to a ball at the palace!' said Ella.
She told me what I have heard in the bakery is
nonsense. 'No, no,' she said. 'It is clear that the
King is looking for a bride for Prince Gabriel. The
prince is, after all, twenty-one years old. It is his
duty to marry and produce an heir.'

Tansy had been bobbing up and down like an
apple in a barrel full of water. 'Can children go

too?' she asked. 'Can they stay up late and dance and eat with the older folk?' It seems that they can.

Ella was swift to say that it was 'the good Miller Trower and family' who are invited. She said that she was Miller Trower's only blood relative and therefore the only one who should go with him. But Papa Miller put a hand on Ella's arm and said very firmly that she was quite wrong. We will all go to the ball.

'Oh,' wailed Ella. 'I shall stand no chance at all of impressing the prince if I am to be with them!' And she pointed rudely at Tansy and Mother and me. Then she clapped her hands to her cheeks and wailed, 'And what can I wear?' She was at once adrift on her familiar stormy sea of hope and despair. She wants gowns and wigs and all sorts, but knows they cannot be afforded.

Miller Trower smiled at Ella for thinking that her whole future life might depend upon one gown! But Ella looked at Papa Miller with wild eyes. 'None of you understands. I must have a new gown! I shall go and see Sally at the drapers right away.'

'But you were going to help me with the washing,' protested Mother.

'How can you think of washing at a time like this?' squealed Ella. 'There is only one week in which to get ready to meet Prince Gabriel!' And she snatched up her hat and hurried, half running, half walking, over the cobbles to the drapers to hear the gossip of fashion there.

'Oh, dear,' said Mother. 'We really cannot afford to have anything made up. And I hardly have the time to make new gowns. If only Ella herself were something of a seamstress. Indeed, I think she is right that she must marry a wealthy man. She has neither the skill nor the patience to look after herself. And what about us, girls?' Mother put one arm around Tansy and one around me. 'What are we going to wear?'

I dislike dressing in my best. Silk stockings and fine cotton garments rip so easily. Their light colours show every mark.

When I am dressed in my best I feel as if I am walking a tightrope. Any clumsy step and I will come to disaster. I am much more at home in my simple everyday clothes. Mother and Tansy and I have the good, if modest, gowns that Mother and I made for her wedding to Miller Trower. Tansy has grown even since then, but we can match the fabric and add to the hem.

Mother's gown is of strawberry print, and mine a simple speckled summer sky-blue. It is decorated with some flowers that I embroidered around the sleeves and neck. Nobody has yet noticed the tiny ladybird and grasshopper I sewed, cunningly hidden amongst them!

Ella had a new gown for the wedding too, a far more elaborate affair than ours. It is yellow and fancy with large bows down its front. But Ella declares that the yellow gown is already out of fashion and she cannot possibly wear it for the ball at the Palace.

That is the trouble with fashion, it seems. It is a race to keep up with the rest, to be the same, but the race is always hurrying onward. Stand still for a moment to enjoy where you are at, and the crowd has gone on without you.

'What food will there be at the party?' is all Tansy can think of.

I told her, 'I expect there will be meringues. There may be syllabubs and even spun sugar baskets of raspberries and cream.'

'And chocolate pies?'

'And chocolate pies.'

Certainly Papa Miller is busy into the night. He is grinding grain to the finest flour, sifting, sifting to get every speck of bran out of it. The flour is for Baker Reuben to cook into the list of dainties that have been ordered by the palace.

2nd April

I have taken Ella's turn at washing the pots yet again. Ella has taken to her bed with a headache. Mother has laid a cloth soaked in vinegar across her forehead to try to ease the pain.

'There's nothing really wrong with her,' I told Mother, and Mother sighed.

'I know that it is not fair on you, Silla, but Ella is unhappy and I'm sorry for the girl.'

'But why?'

Mother took up the drying cloth. 'Ella has persuaded herself that this ball is her one chance to find happiness in a world that has turned against her.'

I laughed.

'I know, I know,' said Mother. 'But remember that she did not want us to move into her home. She did not want Martha to go. She longs for love and marriage so that she can be at the centre of things once again. At present she sees no hope of love beyond that gawky young Alfred at the bakery. And now she has a chance to meet new people at a grand ball.

'There will be fine young men at the ball, and there will be Prince Gabriel himself, of course. But Ella says that she will not even go to the ball unless she has the gown she has set her heart on.'

'And what gown is that? One with great wide skirts, I suppose?'

I had seen the sketches Ella brought back from the drapers.

'Very wide,' smiled Mother. I threw the dish cloth into the water and folded my arms.

'I do not see how she can hope to get close to the man of her dreams in such a thing – it must hold everybody at a distance from her! And you cannot sit down in such a skirt without it springing up in front of you! Why ever does she like it?'

'Because it is the fashion,' said Mother. Then she stroked a hand over my head. 'Silla, Ella's unhappiness makes Thomas unhappy. I feel that I am not a good wife to him if his daughter cannot like me. That is why I would dearly love to give Ella her wish, whatever I think of her taste in gowns. I think that she might begin to like me a little if only I could give her what she wants.'

'Then let us do it!' I said, and I took Mother's hand in mine.

Poor Mother looked so tired and worried, and truly we would all be happier if only Ella can find a way to be happy.

Ella was suspicious when Mother and Tansy and I told her of our plan. 'How can it be afforded?' she asked.

We had that worked out. There will be some money coming from the extra work at the mill on account of the ball, and I have some small savings from my work at the bakery. Alfred and

I made and decorated gingerbread men and sold them at the fair and Baker Reuben let us keep the profit from our work. Ella herself has a little money put aside and even Tansy offered the penny that Papa Miller gave her a while back.

I got paper from the bakery which we use to wrap the fine cakes in, and we borrowed coloured inks from the bookseller next door. Together, around the big table in the kitchen, we designed the dress for Ella to wear to the ball.

She told the shape it must be, with great hooped skirts and a shockingly low front and lots of ribbons. She wanted fabric flaps hanging from the back, but that would need far too much fabric. And she wanted it to be pink, but Mother gently suggested that such a colour might not be flattering should Ella's cheeks blush red as she danced.

'But I will whiten my face,' said Ella. 'All the ladies do.' Mother does not approve of the powder the apothecary sells for this use. She suggests choosing a more flattering colour for the gown: sage green, to set off Ella's golden hair.

'But I should wear a wig, powdered grey or white,' said Ella, but even she can see that we could never make, and could certainly not afford to buy, a wig.

Tansy wants Ella to wear Milksop, the sleepy old mill cat, upon her head instead of a wig! Tansy giggled at the idea, but I told her to hush for fear of upsetting Ella.

'We can pile up your real hair and trim it prettily,' I told Ella. 'It will look finer than any wig.'

'But it will never be trimmed as finely as the grand ladies. They wear sailing boats or gardens in their hair,' said Ella, ready to tip into despair once more. She has been hearing the latest gossip of court fashion for hair at the drapers.

It sounds even sillier to me than Tansy's suggestion of wearing a cat! I shall not attempt anything so ridiculously grand for Ella's hair, but I know that I can make it interesting. When Father was alive, he and I used to make and decorate small surprise presents for Mother and Tansy. I use the same skills in decorating cakes at

the bakery. Baker Reuben often calls on me to trim a cake with almond paste and paper shapes and ribbons for some special occasion. Hair cannot be so very different to decorate.

'You will have butterflies,' I told Ella. 'They will look quite as bright and beautiful as real living ones. We can pin them into your hair and it will look exotic and wonderful.'

'Is it fashionable?' asked Ella in a doubtful voice.

'If the people who see it like it, then it will swiftly become the next fashion,' I told her.

'Oh, yes,' said Tansy. 'Can I have butterflies too, please, Ella?'

I was about to say 'yes', I would make butterflies for all of us, but then I saw Ella's face.

'No, Tansy. The butterflies will only be for Ella.' Ella did not smile, but the frown eased a little.

Then she turned tragic once more and wailed, 'The gown will be of no use at all if I do not have hoops to wear under it! I cannot go to the dance in a droopy gown!'

Mother and I looked at each other, quite lost for ideas. But this time Tansy spoke up. 'You can have my play hoop, if you like.'

3rd April

Mother and Ella bought the shimmering pale green fabric for the dress. Together they spent hours on their hands and knees on the parlour floor, placing paper patterns again and again until they could get the fullest skirt from the yards of fabric they had.

Tansy covered her ears and held her breath as the big sheers sliced into the marvellous cloth.

Mother pinned and Ella tacked the pieces together. Ella pricked her finger and wailed that a drop of blood was on the cloth and all ruined when it was not. Ella has only sewn samplers before and never done workaday sewing, but she is working hard at this.

It is going to take days of stitching before the gown is anywhere near ready. And Ella is wanting trimmings for the gown that Mother really cannot afford. She is also in a fuss that Tansy's hoop is the wrong shape; not the wrong shape for a play hoop, but the wrong shape for a fashionable gown. She says that ladies now wear skirts that stick out more to each side than to the front and back. She has drawn pictures of skirts with hips so wide they look like pack mule panniers!

4th April

I took Tansy with me walking out of town, out into the spring countryside that used to be our home. We talked about Father and the old times in a way that we cannot easily do at the mill. I took a sharp knife with me and we collected lengths of sprouting willow twig. We gathered white goose feathers by a pond and put them into my basket. Then we picked violets and primroses

and put them into the basket too.

'Why not make posies and sell them in town?' suggested Tansy, so we did. We picked pale yellow daffodils from the rough grass beside the road, and we mixed the daffodils with twigs of pussy willow. We tied the posies with grasses twisted together, and walked back to town with our arms full.

Tansy wanted to sell the flowers on her own. The posies were her idea, and people are always more willing to buy from a younger girl.

I took some of the violets and primroses home to crystallize. Very carefully, I dipped each flower in turn into a dish of egg white, and then into a dish of crushed sugar before placing the flowers onto a cloth on the window sill to set hard. The glistening purple and yellow spring flowers will sit prettily on the buns and pies and cakes and biscuits for the royal ball. Purple is a royal colour and will flatter the king. Baker Reuben will be pleased.

Later

Tansy returned home with a pocket full of pennies, and we went together to the haberdashers to choose ribbons and buttons for Ella's dress. We chose mother-of-pearl buttons and moss green velvet ribbons, quite plain but very beautiful.

We spent a long time choosing, both nervous of how Ella would receive the gift.

I told Tansy that she should give them to Ella.

Ella was slumped over the sewing when we found her. Mother was in the kitchen preparing our evening meal. 'Ella,' said Tansy. 'Silla and I have something for you.'

'What manner of something?' asked Ella, pushing back the hair that had tumbled from its fastenings. She eased upright and took the twisted paper cone from Tansy. Her face flickered between a smile and a frown. 'Is it sweet comfits?' she asked.

'Open it and see!'

Tansy clasped her hands together in front of her chest and bit her lip.

'Oh!' said Ella, as the ribbons and buttons fell out. Then she smiled her beautiful smile that we so seldom see. She patted Tansy's arm, and then she looked at me and she said, 'Thank you.'

5th April

We have all been so busy today. Mother and Ella are still stitching the dress. Papa Miller took the willow twigs that Tansy and I brought home. He soaked them to softness, then bent and twisted them together and arranged them around the wash tub so that they would dry in the shape we wanted.

Papa Miller was worried that the twigs would never dry in time, but Alfred came to the rescue. He sneaked the tubs into the warmth of the bakery after Baker Reuben had left for the night. The twigs should dry overnight and stiffen into smooth hoops, just the shape Ella wants for her skirts.

Tansy has spent all day in the window seat. She has her tongue between her teeth in concentration as her small fingers cut and sew tiny flower heads and leaves in the shapes of primroses and violets. Ella has no notion yet that her gown will match the dainty foods at the ball!

I have been out in the yard making butterflies. I cut wings from the tips of the goose feathers and coloured them with a flour paste mixed with ground colours. I used thread to fasten the wings to tiny twig bodies, and I wired glass beads to be eyes on long stalks.

Mother put her hands to her cheeks when she

saw the state of me, but she cheered when she saw the butterflies. 'So real, they could flap those wings and fly away,' she said.

Even Ella says that they are pretty, though she looked at my colour-blotched hands with distaste.

6th April

It now seems that we have achieved what seemed impossible six days ago. Ella's gown shall be finished tomorrow after all, and Ella shall go to the ball. For a moment she seemed content. She even thanked Mother. She said that a fairy godmother could not have magicked a more marvellous gown.

Later, by candlelight

Ella soon found more to make her despair. She asks, how can she shine in her gown when she will be seen with us in our plain outfits? 'The grand folk will turn their backs when they see the company I keep,' she said. 'You will drag me down!'

I wanted to punch her pretty nose when she said that, but I simply left the room and came upstairs to write in this book. I shall hold back one of the butterflies and Tansy shall have one in her hair after all!

Mother does not yet know it, but I have used coloured wax and green paper to make tiny strawberries to adorn her hair and match her gown. I look forward to seeing her face tomorrow.

Meanwhile, even from up here, I can still hear Ella wailing, 'And we have no coach to take us to the ball as the better people do. Oh, Papa, we must arrange to borrow one. And I have no shoes to wear! Mine are old and dull and not at all suited to my new gown.' As Ella carries on, Papa Miller says, 'There, there, my dear. We will think of something. Do not despair so. You shall look fine and dandy and arrive at the ball in brilliant style.'

How can he be so patient with her? He is sometimes a little too kind, I think.

7th April

It is the day of the ball. I have been helping at the bakery, trimming the cakes and fancies with my violets and primroses and slivered toasted almonds and coloured sugars. Baker Reuben himself gilded the gingerbread with gold leaf. It was very pleasing to see the trays of bakings, covered in linen and being taken on wagons towards the palace and to know that I have had a part in creating the pretty things. I only hope I can fit into the waist of my gown tonight. Alfred and I have feasted on all kinds of cakes and broken biscuits that were not perfect enough for the palace.

By way of payment for today's work, I asked Baker Reuben for the scraps of gold leaf left over from his gilding. I shall add a golden sparkle to my butterflies. There are still some hours to go before the ball, but the mill house is loud with excited chatter already as we prepare. Mother is brushing and brushing Tansy's hair with vinegar on the brush to make her hair shine.

Ella is in a sulk because Mother has told her she has to iron her gown herself. You never heard such a fuss. 'I cannot do it! Oh, it will all be ruined!' I know that Martha used to do all the washing and ironing. I doubt Ella has ever tried it before. She must have let the iron go cold and forgotten to take a fresh hot one from the fire.

I may go and help her in a little while, but I shall get my own gown and stockings and

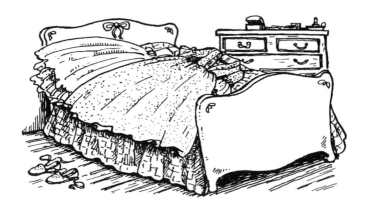

petticoats laid out and ready first. I'm fond of my gown. I chose the speckled fabric because it looks to me exactly as though a mouse has put his paws into a dish of ink and scurried all over it.

Later

After hours of preparation, we are all finally ready. Papa Miller wears a handsome tail coat, silk stockings and breeches, and not a speck of flour dust on him. He looks ruddy as a pippin apple, hot and uncomfortable. But he says that he is thoroughly proud of what he calls his 'four fine ladies'.

Ella humphed when he said that. It is no surprise that she thinks that she is looking fine, but she can hardly bear to glance at Mother and Tansy and me.

Mother managed to pile Ella's hair almost as high as a wig. She placed her pin cushion (having taken out all the pins) onto Ella's head. Then she brought the hair up around it and twisted it to hide the pin cushion altogether. Mother and I wired and pinned the butterflies through it to tie everything in place.

The butterflies do look lovely, their golden speckled wings glinting amongst her golden hair. It is a shame that Ella insists on dulling her hair by powdering it with Papa Miller's finest flour.

I saw her dab a little flour onto her face too, to make it paler, and she squashed a berry between two fingers and used the juice to redden her lips and cheeks. She has to hold her head very still and a little stiff, but she is pleased with what she sees in her looking glass, and that is a relief to us all.

Ella's new gown does look fine, even though it is so wide that Ella has to shuffle sideways to

get through the door. She has to shuffle in any case because there is another problem that is stopping her from walking properly – her shoes. Ella has glass slippers on her feet! Whoever heard of such a thing?

She saw them in a shop window and sold her dead mama's jewels in order to buy them. Mother put a hand over her mouth when she saw the shoes, unsure whether to laugh at their silliness or cry for the waste of money.

'They surely cannot be intended for wearing, Ella. I am certain they must have been meant only for display, for glass does not bend. Nobody could walk in those!'

But Ella knows better. 'I am sure that all the grand ladies wear them,' she said, and she has put them on. It makes me wince to look at her, but she is quite determined.

How glad I am for my soft cotton gown and comfortable leather slippers.

My hair is twisted and trimmed too, but not so high. I can move with ease. Mother pinned a small posy of violets to my dress, and their smell reminds me what an exceptional night we are about to experience: a ball at the palace! Mother is delighted with the strawberries in her brown hair, and the gilded butterfly looks wonderful in Tansy's.

Alfred has kindly offered to drive us to the palace in our mill wagon, so we shall arrive almost like grand folk. I think poor Alfred is a

little jealous of us going to the ball. I have promised to remember every detail and tell him all about it tomorrow.

He has cleaned out the wagon specially. There are quilts laid inside it so that we shall not soil our smart clothes. And Alfred has brushed and braided and beribboned Bess, the horse, to splendour. The wagon is here now, with Alfred smiling adoringly at Ella. She, of course, scornfully turns away from poor nice Alfred. But we are ready to go!

After midnight

What a night of magnificence and surprises! When Alfred held out a hand to help Ella into the wagon, Ella suddenly declared that she simply could not be seen arriving at the ball in a dusty miller's cart with her stepmother and ugly stepsisters. She demanded that her papa must leave us behind and take only her to the ball.

Poor Papa Miller! He was in such a scarlet state of alarm. He was angry with Ella for saying such things, yet desperate to console his unhappy beautiful daughter.

What could he do? To my surprise, Papa Miller came down firmly on our side. So, as Ella stood in sullen shock, the four of us climbed

into the wagon and trotted off to the ball without her. I am sure that she had not expected that. Alone on the mill doorstep, she shrank smaller and smaller as we sped down the road towards the palace.

I think that each one of us felt as forlorn as she did, after all the effort of the last week to send her happy to the ball. Mother said that we must turn back for Ella. She said that she herself would not mind staying at home if it would make Ella happy. But Papa Miller said that we must forget about the silly girl and not let her spoil our evening. He promised to dance with each of us three young ladies in turn.

The palace was dazzling. So many flaring torches lighting the driveway! Such a size of a place! So much music and laughter spilling out of the windows!

Tansy clasped my hand and I could feel that she was fizzing with excitement, just as I was. There were grand folk, sweeping up the gravel drive in handsome shining carriages with footmen riding behind ready to open the doors and hand the ladies down the steps. But none of them to my mind had a horse to pull them as jolly as our Bess, with her mane and tail plaited with ribbons and strung with bells.

The King, Queen and Prince Gabriel greeted all as we entered the ballroom, and a man with a great voice shouted out our names, 'Miller and Mrs Thomas Trower and daughters, Druscilla and Anastasia!'

Those names didn't feel as if they were ours, but they were!

Tansy stood with her mouth open as the King himself shook Papa Miller's hand just as firmly as he shook those of the big wigs.

The Queen smiled beautifully at everyone, and Prince Gabriel stood, tall and handsome, with a charmingly lonely look in his eyes. He bent down graciously to compliment Tansy on the golden butterfly in her hair. Then he pointed us towards the tables laden with drinks and food.

The tarts and buns and fancies that I had helped to prepare were displayed amongst fruit and flowers and meats and pies and puddings and shining silver and candles all over a white damask table cloth. It was all quite beautiful and made me feel tremendously hungry!

While Papa Miller introduced Mother to other gentlemen he knew, Tansy and I walked around.

We looked and looked at the marvellous outfits worn by the grander folk, and it was fun spotting whose wigs were beginning to slip.

A string quartet played in one corner of the ballroom, but they soon made way for a full band with horns and trumpets. When the band played, the ballroom with its domed ceiling rang like a bell.

Conversation became impossible and the people hushed and moved to the sides of the room.

His Majesty the King strode to the middle of the floor. He made a short speech about how glad he was to introduce his son to his people and his people to his son. Then he raised his hands in the air and declared, 'And now it is time to dance!'

'Hooray!' we all cheered, and then there was a gasp. Somebody was stumbling through the door and would have fallen to the floor if Prince Gabriel had not stepped forward to catch her. That someone was Ella! She had stumbled in her glass slippers.

I was aghast, but I need not have worried. As Prince Gabriel helped Ella back onto her feet, his eyes smiled into hers. She blushed through the flour on her cheeks and smiled back at him.

And then the music started and the floor was soon aswirl with skirts and flying jacket tails, and somewhere in the middle of it all, Ella danced with the royal prince. How could she dance in those shoes?

Some time later I noticed one glass slipper tumbled at the side of the room. She must have kicked them off and danced on toes covered only in silk.

Certainly she glided along like a skater. Prince Gabriel was not the only young man to look at her and smile. But Ella danced only with Gabriel.

I danced at the ball too, with Papa Miller and with Tansy and even with one young gentleman.

The young gentleman and Tansy and I ate brandy snap baskets full of cream strewn with my candied flowers. The young man admired the decorations on the food, and Tansy told him of my part in their creation, and about the butterflies.

He asked if he might use my ideas to decorate parties at his parents' great house. Of course I said 'yes', so perhaps Ella's trimmings may become a fashion after all!

Mother and Papa Miller looked so happy, dancing together, enjoying the food and music and bright company. Tansy was petted by all the old ladies, and Ella looked like a true princess as she spun around the floor, even as her hair began to tumble from its perch on her head. Somehow she looked all the more lovely for not looking perfect. I wanted to tell her that she looked beautiful, to show her that I was glad that she had come to the ball, but whenever I came near her, she turned away.

I realized then that she thought that Prince Gabriel might scorn her if he thought her to be related to the humble miller and his family. My mood of goodwill towards Ella soon shrank. She is no better than any of us, for all her willow stick hoops and dots of soot on her cheek and flour in her hair. It was us, her 'frumpy' stepmother and 'ugly' sisters, who had made her the wonderful gown she now wore!

When the time came for us to leave the party, all of us happily weary, we moved towards Ella to include her in the trip home. She was sitting,

gazing out over the moonlit garden with Prince Gabriel by her side and her stockinged toes peeping out from under her skirt.

Mother tapped her on her shoulder. 'Ella, my dear, it is time to go.' But Ella turned and looked with horror at Mother's homely face that had grown a little red and shiny with the exertion of dancing.

'Is this your family?' asked Prince Gabriel.

'No!' said Ella. 'That woman and her girls are nothing to do with me!'

There was a moment of silence. Ella saw at once that her rudeness had shocked the prince. She sobbed out loud and, with tears streaking down her floury face, she leapt up and ran, back through the ballroom and away. Prince Gabriel and I tried to follow. I called her to come back and ride home in the wagon with us, but she was gone.

Poor Prince Gabriel looked distraught. 'Did I upset her in some way?' he asked me.

'No,' I told him. 'It was Ella who upset us all.'

'But,' said the prince, his forehead crinkled with worry, 'she was so happy before, and then so very upset! Might I call upon your family tomorrow and try to make friends with her once more?'

I knew that Ella would be horrified by the thought of the prince seeing inside her home. But, I thought, if there is to be love, then the prince must see Ella for the person she really is. So it was for the sake of the prince as well as to get my revenge on Ella that I smiled and said, 'I'm sure that she would be happy to see you, your Highness. We live at the mill in Corn Hill Street.'

Let the prince see how Ella is at home!

8th April

We all slept late this morning. Papa Miller's apprentice woke the mill for him and the stones were grinding by the time I opened my eyes. Over a late breakfast, Mother, Papa Miller, Tansy and I talked over the wonders of last night – the music and flowers and thousands of candles, the food and the dancing.

In low voices we laughed at the way Ella had made her entrance. Mother found out that, after we left her on the doorstep, Ella begged a lift to the palace and arrived perched on a cart full of pumpkins! I don't know why she thought that was better than arriving in the mill wagon at the correct time in our company!

Mother stayed up long after we got home last night. She was waiting for Ella to come home. Ella finally appeared, wet and bedraggled and the gown we had taken such pains over quite ruined and in rags. She had walked home in stockinged feet, her hair lopsided and dampened with drizzle, her face pink and puffy with crying and her hands clutching one of her glass slippers. Mother had offered warm milk and honey, but Ella had stormed up to her attic room and had not been seen since.

I do not think that any of us felt in any hurry to wake her this morning. Her mood would dull us, and for the present we were happy rekindling

memories of last night, and not thinking of its less happy ending.

We were still at breakfast when there was a knocking at the door. I opened the door to find Prince Gabriel on the doorstep! I didn't know whether to curtsey or speak, or usher him in, or what to do.

I'm afraid that I simply stood there, silent and stupid. I had not really believed that a royal prince would come visiting, yet here he was. And in his hands was one of Ella's glass slippers, cradled as if it were something very precious.

'Might I see Ella?' asked the prince, not at all grandly. 'You see, I have brought her back her shoe.'

Mother was at the door now, patting her hair and tweaking at her workaday gown. 'Oh, your Highness! You are too kind!' She held out a hand. 'I will see that Ella gets the slipper.' But the prince shuffled uneasily and I knew that he wanted to give the slipper to Ella himself.

There was a pause when nobody seemed to know what to say, but I noticed how the prince's eyes were round and shiny as a dog's when it has the hope of a bone. I thought that poor Prince Gabriel had better see the real Ella for himself before he swooned too much into love with her.

'Do come into our drawing room,' I said to him. 'I will fetch Ella down for you.'

So, while Mother shuffled backwards, bobbing up and down in little bows like a pecking hen, with Tansy peeking around the kitchen door and Papa Miller clearing his throat and trying a speech about last night's rain seeming to have cleared, the prince moved into the drawing room. And I ran up the stairs.

'Ella!' I called up the attic steps. 'You are to come down at once!'

'Why?' grumped Ella from her room.

'You will see why soon enough.'

Ella slumped down the stairs, grumbling and scratching at her matted hair which must have been itching full of last night's flour. I am sure that she thought that Mother was going to make her peel potatoes or some such. She thumped down the steps, then she came around the drawing room door and saw Prince Gabriel standing there in his beautiful brown velvet jacket and her mouth dropped open in surprise.

I am afraid that I laughed out loud. Ella was still in her tattered gown from last night, her hair tumbled in knots and butterflies over a face smeared with flour and the sooty beauty spot and tears and rain. I looked for horror on the royal face, but saw only anguish. I looked for humility on Ella's, and saw despair.

Suddenly, I realized the cruelty of what I had done. I froze cold as ice inside and wished with all my heart that I could undo the shame that I had brought upon my sister and my family. Ella tried to turn and run back up the stairs, but Prince Gabriel held her arm.

'I brought your shoe back, Ella.' He wasn't laughing. He was looking at her tenderly.

'Oh!' whispered Ella. 'I'm, I'm . . .' She waved her hands up and down her tattered gown and her hair and she shook her head. Then she looked at Mother and Tansy and me and her face went hard.

She pointed at us. 'It's them,' she said. 'My stepmother and my ugly sisters. They did this to me! They make me sleep in the attic and clean the dirty grates and they laugh at me and, and . . .' Prince Gabriel was smiling and gently guiding Ella to sit down on a chair.

'Ella, Ella!' he said. 'That is all nonsense, and you know it. You have a fine family. I like them; but I love you the best of all. I love your romantic dreams and your passion for beauty.'

He wiped a finger over Ella's cheek where the black beauty spot had smeared, and he chuckled. 'Why, you look as if you have been cleaning cinders from the chimney! I shall call you Cinderella!'

And, do you know? Ella laughed when he said that. She laughed to be teased! It was wonderful. And the prince went on, 'You were so beautiful last night, Ella, and you are beautiful now. Frills and flounces, smudges and tatters, it makes no difference to me. It is you yourself who are beautiful.

'Now, if you would care to tidy yourself, and if your mother will give her permission, I would like to take you out walking. Then we can talk and become better acquainted.'

Ella opened her mouth to speak. I could guess that she was about to declare that Mother was not her mother and never would be, but she caught the smile in Gabriel's eyes and said nothing. Instead, she hurried up to her room and Mother followed her up.

Papa Miller talked to Prince Gabriel while I made a pot of our precious tea, usually brought out only for birthdays and Christmas. Then Ella appeared in her plain blue dress and proper shoes and her hair its own colour, simply twisted on top. She moved naturally in the comfortable clothes, and Gabriel smiled and stood up as she entered the room. I could tell that he liked her even better without the trimmings.

'There now,' said Mother as Ella and Prince Gabriel walked off down the street, arm in arm. 'Isn't that nice.'

2nd June

Ella and Prince Gabriel were married yesterday. The whole town came out onto the streets to see and cheer and sing and join the party as the King's son married the miller's daughter.

'A step or two up in the world for her,' I heard somebody say. Indeed it is, and it is what she had set her heart on. But Prince Gabriel seems just as happy to have taken a step or two down the social ladder. He has a wife with a passionate temper that he finds refreshing after the prim and proper stiff ladies that he knows from court.

Prince Gabriel has an easy fondness and interest for people of all kinds and will, I think, make a very good king when the time comes.

And Ella will be his Queen!

As a bride, Ella wore a pale golden gown with tight sleeves that cascaded into lace below the elbows and a froth of lace around the neck. The skirt was held out by starched petticoats, but no hoop. It was possible for her to sit elegantly in the royal carriage that carried her to and from church.

Her hair was pinned high on her head, but it was allowed to be its own shiny golden colour. It was decorated with fresh flowers and tiny birds with coloured wings that Tansy and I had made. Ella looked so glorious, the crowd gasped and cheered as the carriage passed by. Tansy and I were flower girls. We rode in the carriages too.

A good number of the smarter lady guests at the wedding were wearing stiffly hooped skirts and butterflies in their hair. Mother caught my eye and winked!

Papa Miller stood beside Ella to give her away, pride pinking his cheeks. He and Baker Reuben and Alfred and I have created the most wonderful bride cake, seven tiers high. It has

almond paste and sugar icing and sugar flowers and hearts all over. Nobody has yet spotted the paste ladybird that Alfred and I hid amongst the flowers!

There was a glorious party after the wedding, and we went home happy, leaving Ella with her prince. Mother says that Ella has finally grown up. 'It was clear today,' she said. 'All those ladies tripping over themselves to dress as Ella had dressed at the ball. They all suppose that if only they can look like that, then they, too, will win the heart of a prince!'

'I saw one lady with strawberries in her hair,' I told Mother. 'Perhaps she wants to become mother-in-law to a prince. That makes you a leader of fashion just as much as Ella!'

Mother chuckled, then said, 'Our Ella was looking delightfully different today. She has the confidence to choose for herself and lead others. Her days of unhappily stumbling along behind what others say she should wear are gone. I am very proud of her.' Miller gave Mother a big hug and a kiss on the lips when she said that about his Ella. He said that he was proud of all his girls. And I realize with some surprise that I am proud of both my fathers and my sisters too. I really am happy.

And Ella? She will always be wanting the next thing, but I think that she will choose those things for herself now. The very next thing she wants is a baby, so it is as well that Mother declares her to be grown up!

The
Strange World
of Cinderella

The Strange World of Cinderella

In books, pantomimes and films, the story of *Cinderella* always seems to be set in the days when it was fashionable to wear great powdered wigs and huge elaborate skirts. Those were the fashions during the eighteenth century, so I have set *Sister Ella* loosely in that time.

Fashion

Nowadays only some lawyers wear stiff wigs of grey curls, but there was a time when all fashionable rich people wore them. The more important or wealthy the people were, the

bigger their wigs and that is why they were known as 'big wigs'.

They really did powder their hair with flour. Even young people wanted their wigs to look grey or white like an old person's hair.

They would pile their hair up over metal frames and padding, and then decorate it with feathers, ribbons and flowers. Some sat for hours while hairdressers 'dressed' their hair, putting model ships or cottages or almost anything into it to create a beautiful scene.

Hats were also fashionable. Poorer people made their own caps and bonnets, but those who could afford it bought elaborate hats, decorated by people called 'milliners'. The name milliner comes from the Italian town of Milan, which was famous for making hats. In my story, Ella's stepmother thought that fashion-conscious Ella might enjoy being a milliner.

Skirts became very big in the eighteenth century. Some skirts stuck out sideways for as much as a metre each side. Ladies wearing those skirts couldn't fit through most doorways unless they turned sideways. If you look at grand houses built at that time, they often have very wide doorways to let the ladies fit through. I suppose that wearing clothes that prevented you from being able to do anything practical was a sign of how rich you were.

Men's fashion was also very grand. Some gentlemen wore high-heeled shoes, breeches, stockings and tailed jackets.

It was fashionable for men to wear ribbons around their necks and in their hair. Some of them whitened their faces and reddened their lips with make-up.

Some even wore black beauty spots, just as the ladies did. They bought their make-up from an apothecary's shop, the equivalent of our modern chemist shops.

Apothecaries sold medicines, but they also sold things to help you look beautiful. Ella's stepmother was quite right to dislike the powder they sold for whitening faces. It was made from

lead and was poisonous. Over time, it ate into the skin of people who used it and made holes in their skin – not very beautiful! It could also affect people's brains and make them mad.

In the eighteenth century you couldn't go and buy clothes from shops in the way that we do. Every item of clothing was specially made. There were no sewing machines so everything was hand stitched. People might get ideas from seeing what others wore or from looking in fashion journals. Then they would copy or adapt those ideas for their own clothes.

It could take weeks or even months to make and embroider the finest jackets and dresses. So the whole process of fashion was much slower than it is today.

You chose and bought the fabric for your

clothes from a draper's shop. You got pins, ribbons and buttons from a haberdasher.

Paper patterns were made to work out the shapes to cut from the fabric. Fabric was very expensive and must not be wasted. The rich were showing off their wealth when they used lots of fabric for their enormous skirts and lengths of cloth they liked to drape from dress shoulders.

Once fabric had been cut, the seams were pinned and then tacked (sewn loosely with big stitches). The tacked garment could be tried on and adjusted to fit before the seams were finally sewn with tiny neat stitches. A woman who did that fine sewing was called a seamstress.

How do we know what people wore two hundred years ago? There are some examples of the finest clothes from the time on display in museums. There are wonderful eighteenth century coats and dresses in the Victoria and Albert Museum in London.

What else? Of course there are no photographs from that time, but it was fashionable for rich people to have pictures

painted of themselves. Families posed, dressed in their best in a pretty country setting or with their grand house behind them. If you look in an art gallery you might find some of those paintings.

There was also a fashion for tiny painted portraits called miniatures. There are fewer clues to how poorer people dressed, but artists such as William Hogarth included ordinary people in their drawings and paintings.

Every-day life

Food

Two hundred years ago most people grew the food they needed to feed themselves. They took their harvest of grain to be ground at a local mill. It might have been a windmill or a mill that was powered by a waterwheel in a stream or a river.

The grain was ground to flour between huge stones. The ordinary flour still had bits of bran in it, but more expensive flour was sifted again and again to make it finer and whiter. Only the richer people could afford white bread. These days we know that it is healthier to eat brown bread. We even buy bread with extra bran added to it. Food, too, goes in fashions!

Many people didn't have an oven at home, so they would bring their food to be put into the baker's big oven. The baker also made bread and cakes to sell. For special occasions, bakers really did decorate gingerbread with gold, hammered very thin into gold leaf. Putting gold onto something is called 'gilding'.

Baking was hard work. Each raisin had to be washed and its stalk and pips removed.

Sugar came in great conical solid 'loaves' which had to be crushed or grated into loose sugar before it could be used.

In the story Tansy looks forward to eating

meringues. The egg whites for those meringues would have been beaten with a fork by hand. There were no mechanical mixers to speed things up. The cook's arm would have been as stiff as the egg whites by the time they were ready for baking into meringues!

Tansy was also excited by the thought of chocolate pies. Chocolate was still quite new in Britain at that time. Nobody had yet invented the bars of chocolate we are familiar with today. Cocoa beans were brought from Central America and then ground into cocoa powder. That powder could then be made into a drink or used for cooking.

Chocolate was expensive and thought of as being rather a daring thing to drink.

Coffee was another fashionable drink. Coffee houses were places where people who could afford it would meet and drink and talk.

Tea was also something new and special. It was so precious that it was kept in locked tea caddies and only the mistress of the house would have the key.

Houses

Wealthy people with large houses had a drawing room for sitting in, or entertaining visitors. Originally, it was a *with*drawing room. The ladies withdrew there after dinner while the men stayed behind to drink and smoke. The only heating for houses was from open fires. Each morning the cinders left from the previous day's fire had to be cleared, and a fresh fire started.

Travel

Most eighteenth century roads were just muddy tracks through the countryside. People rode horses, walked, or travelled in horse-drawn carriages, but most never went far because travel was difficult and could be dangerous. Highwaymen lurked on some of the more remote roads, waiting to rob travellers.

Some town streets were cobbled, but that still didn't make travelling comfortable. There were no rubber tyres filled with air to cushion the bumps, only solid wheels.

Smart people wanting to travel just a short distance might have chosen to be carried in a sedan chair. A sedan chair was a kind of box carried on poles by two strong men. They can't have been very comfortable to ride in either, but at least it kept your shoes and the bottom of your long skirts out of the mud.

The streets were often dirty and ladies and gentlemen sometimes clutched a posy (a small bunch) of violets or other scented flowers to hide the smells around them.

Miller Trower had a horse-drawn wagon to carry his sacks of grain and flour, but goods going long distances were often taken by pack horse or pony with pannier bags slung over their backs.

Children

Most eighteenth century children never went to school. They had to help their parents and work, and they probably never learnt to read or write. Children of wealthier parents sometimes had lessons at home, perhaps from their mother or

from a tutor. There were some schools for boys, and there were small 'dame schools' where any child who paid could go for a few years.

Children didn't have as many toys as they do nowadays. They might, like Tansy, have had a hoop to play with or perhaps a doll or rattle. Toys go in fashions too. There is a picture of a fashionable lady in 1791 playing with a yoyo!

Lucky children might be bought 'sweet comfits' for a treat. Sweet comfits were sweets made from fruits or nuts dipped in sugary syrup. So, if someone calls you a 'sugar plum', it means that they think you are sweet!

In some ways eighteenth century life was the

way I have shown it in my story. But, of course, there never was a real King Gabriel and Queen Ella. I don't think any real eighteenth century king would have invited the miller and his family to a grand ball. And nobody would ever have really arrived at the door of a king's palace on a cart full of pumpkins; but this is a story, and the wonderful thing about stories is that you can make anything you like happen in them, whether or not they would ever happen in real life!

About the Author

Most of the characters in the old fairy stories are either completely good or completely bad. Cinderella is good, and her sisters bad. In real life, of course, we're all a mixture of both. I've always felt sorry for those 'ugly' sisters with the 'beautiful' stepsister who is loved by everyone, including the Prince. That's why I decided to let one of them tell the story from her point of view for a change. But I hope that you will find yourself liking them all by the end!